AROUND THE CLOCK!

ROZ CHAST

Atheneum Books for Young Readers

New York London Toronto Sydney New Dehli

ATHENEUM BOOKS FOR YOUNG READERS
An imprint of Simon & Schuster Children's Publishing Division
1230 Avenue of the Americas, New York, New York 10020
Copyright © 2015 by Roz Chast
All rights reserved, including the right of reproduction in whole or
in part in any form.
ATHENEUM BOOKS FOR YOUNG READERS is a registered trademark
of Simon & Schuster, Inc.
Atheneum logo is a trademark of Simon & Schuster, Inc.
For information about special discounts for bulk purchases,
please contact Simon & Schuster Special Sales at 1-866-506-1949
or business@simonandschuster.com.
The Simon & Schuster Speakers Bureau can bring authors to your
live event. For more information or to book an event, contact the
Simon & Schuster Speakers Bureau at 1-866-248-3049 or visit our
website at www.simonspeakers.com.
The text for this book is set in Caecilia LT Std.
The illustrations for this book are rendered in ink and watercolor.
Manufactured in China
1014 SCP
First Edition
10 9 8 7 6 5 4 3 2 1
Library of Congress Cataloging-in-Publication Data
Chast, Roz, author, illustrator.
Around the clock / Roz Chast.—First edition.
p. cm

Summary: "Do you ever wonder what your friends, enemies,
brothers, sisters, and children are doing in the hours when
you're not there? This kooky 24-hour tour of a day in the life of
23 different children will reveal answers you'd never expect"—
Provided by publisher.

ISBN 978-1-4169-8476-4 (hc)—ISBN 978-1-4424-9689-7 (eBook)
[1. Stories in rhyme. 2. Day—Fiction.
3. Imagination—Fiction. 4. Humorous stories.]
I. Title.
PZ8.3.C389Aro 2015
[E]—dc23
2013050716

From 6 to 7,
Pete is up,
drinking from
his favorite cup.

From 7 to 8,
Billy's muse
tells him to paint
the room
chartreuse.

From 8 to 9, Bea likes to see
her favorite program on TV.

From 9 to 10, Deb has forgotten:
Are unicorns real, or are they notten?

From 10 to 11, Hazel Jane
puts one hundred marbles down the drain.

From 11 to 12, Lou is snoring.
That's because his life is boring.

From 12 to 1, Lynn eats baloney
with her imaginary friend, Tony.

From 1 to 2, in his fanciest pants,
Don is digging a hole to France.

From 2 to 3, Ian's in school.
Long division can be so cruel.

From 3 to 4,
in the grocery store,
Ann throws a tantrum
on the floor.

From 4 to 5, Patty's in luck:
here comes a Frozen Toastee truck!

From 5 to 6, Steve is able
to help his mother set the table.

From 6 to 7, Sophie cries.
That's because dinner is Liver Surprise.

From 7 to 8 is bath time for Shelley.
If you don't take a bath, you will get very smelly.

From 8 to 9, please observe Ricky:
Why does his toothpaste taste so icky?

From 9 to 10, Lynn can't understand
why someone would knit pajamas by hand.

From 10 to 11, it's the worst—
poor little Emma is dying of thirst!

From 11 to 12, though no one can see him,
Dave is planning a sock museum.

From 12 to 1,
Jill dreams she can fly.

From 1 to 2, small John Paul
worries about wires in the wall.

From 2 to 3, Andy's awake,
having some milk and a morsel of cake.

From 3 to 4, Ellis becomes
"ELL-MAN, Master of Bongo Drums."

From 4 to 5, you'll see June
in a garden she grows by the light of the moon.

but when he wakes up . . .

. . . they all disappear.